Caring for Your
Mouse

Tamar Lupo

Weigl Publishers Inc.

Project Coordinator
Heather C. Hudak

Design
Warren Clark

Published by Weigl Publishers Inc.
350 5th Avenue, Suite 3304, PMB 6G
New York, NY 10118-0069
Web site: www.weigl.com

Library of Congress Cataloging-in-Publication Data

Lupo, Tamar.
  Caring for your mouse / Tamar Lupo.
     p. cm. -- (Caring for your pet)
  Includes index.
  ISBN 1-59036-472-4 (lib. bd. : alk. paper) -- ISBN 1-59036-473-2 (soft cover : alk. paper)
  1. Mice as pets--Juvenile literature. I. Title. II. Series: Caring for your pet (Mankato, Minn.)
  SF459.M5L87 2007
  636.935'3--dc22

                         2006016102

                  Printed in the United States of America
                  1 2 3 4 5 6 7 8 9 0   10 09 08 07 06

Locate the mouse paw prints throughout the book to find useful tips on caring for your pet.

Photograph and Text Credits
Every reasonable effort has been made to trace ownership and to obtain permission to reprint copyright material. The publishers would be pleased to have any errors or omissions brought to their attention so that they may be corrected in subsequent printings.

Cover: Berries can be healthy for a mouse to eat.

All of the Internet URLs given in the book were valid at the time of publication. However, due to the dynamic nature of the Internet, some addresses may have changed, or sites may have ceased to exist since publication. While the author and publisher regret any inconvenience this may cause readers, no responsibility for any such changes can be accepted by either the author or the publisher.

Contents

Mouse Musings

Mice have been around for thousands of years. They can be found in every part of the world. The mouse is very **nimble**. It is able to jump and climb, using its tail to balance and grip. Mice are also very curious. Mice are nocturnal, so they are most active in the evening.

In the past, mice were thought to be pests because they ate crops. Some mice carried diseases, too. Over time, people found that mice could also make good pets. Having a small "pocket" pet is a good way to learn about being a responsible pet owner. However, a first-time mouse owner should be 8 years of age or older.

Do not buy a mouse that has bald patches. This likely is a sign that he is ill.

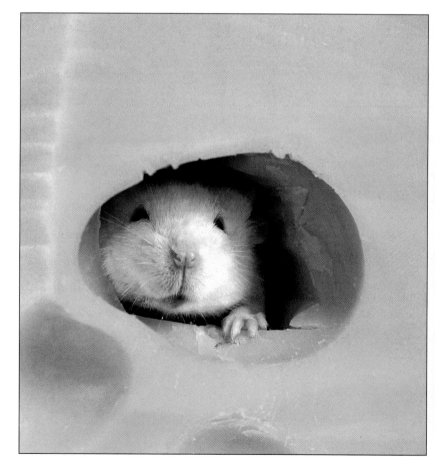

■ The traditional house mouse weighs between 0.4 and 1.1 ounces (12 and 30 grams).

Although mice are small, they are still a big responsibility. They need exercise, food, water, and a place to nest. They also need to be handled carefully. A new mouse friend will need a few days to become used to his new home. Do not pick him up right away. Let him smell your hand and nibble food from your fingers. You can also lightly stroke his fur. Do not startle your new pet by making sudden movements. Once the mouse gets to know you, he will be a good-natured and wonderful friend.

A pet mouse should be handled for at least a half hour each day.

Fascinating Facts

- Male mice are called bucks. Female mice are called does. Baby mice are pups or pinkies.
- Baby mice will curl up when they are carried in a person's hand.
- Mice will stand on their hind legs to get a good view of the objects around them.

Pet Profiles

There are many different **species** of mice around the world. Striped, deer, wood, harvest, and spiny are a few of the mice species found in nature. Most **domesticated** mice are fancy mice. They are bred for show. Fancy mice have special features, such as silky satin coats, wavy hair, and curly whiskers.

LONG HAIR

- Has long, shiny, satiny hair
- Bred to be shown in competitions
- Ears tend to be smaller than those of other mice

SELF DOVE

- Has a light gray coat with no other markings
- This color occurs when champagne-colored mice are bred with black mice
- Has pink eyes
- Fur on the belly is not as thick as the fur on the back

SATIN

- Has a glossy, satin-like coat
- Comes in many colors, such as dove (gray), fawn (deep tan), ivory (off-white), argente (silvery), or champagne (pinkish)

The most common domesticated mouse is the house mouse. In nature, house mice have a brown coat with some black hair sprinkled throughout. However, pet house mice come in many different colors, such as black, chocolate, gray, silver, and white. Some even have spots or patches of many colors.

PIEBALD

- Has a white coat with many different colored patches, called marks
- The broken mark and the Dutch mark are two types of piebald mice
- Piebald marks also occur on rabbits, horses, and small **livestock**

STRIPED

- Only found in nature; not sold as pets
- Has brown fur with four black stripes down the back
- Has two to nine pups in a **litter**
- Grows to be double the size of a house mouse

ALBINO

- Has completely white hair and red eyes
- Used for science and medical research
- Sometimes sold as pets
- Bred in Japan more than 300 years ago

Mouse Memoirs

Mice have lived on Earth for millions of years. House mice have lived among humans for more than 8,000 years. Humans were hunter gatherers. They collected and stored food and grains. Mice began eating these food stores.

Mice first appeared in books in China around 1,100 B.C. In the 1700s, people began keeping white mice as pets in Japan. Settlers brought some of these mice to Europe in the 1800s. Keeping fancy mice as pets became very popular in Great Britain.

Over time, people began bringing mice to North America. A U.S. pet care book in the 1920s talked about keeping mice as pets.

Mice are very curious. They will search their surroundings daily for any changes.

Over many years, mice became more common than they were long ago. In the 1950s, the American Mouse Club was founded to set breed standards and host shows. Today, there are many mouse clubs in the United States and around the world.

Since the 1990s, mice have become very common pets. Many people kept reptiles as pets. These people bought mice to feed their reptiles, but they soon learned that mice made great pets, too.

Mice found in nature do not make good pets. They are aggressive and sometimes carry disease. It is best to buy a mouse from a pet store or breeder.

Mice try to keep within 12 and 20 feet (3.7 and 6.1 meters) of their nest.

Fascinating Facts

- Waltzing or dancing mice are very small, and they often cannot hear. Their lack of hearing causes them to have poor balance, so they spin around in circles instead of walking.
- Many mice were brought to North America as **stowaways** on ships or in people's luggage.

Life Cycle

It is exciting to bring home a cute, furry mouse. Your new pet will depend on you for food, shelter, and attention. Like all pets, your mouse will need different things at various stages of its life.

Newborn Mouse

Baby mice are pink, smooth, and hairless. They are the size of a human fingertip. Their ears and eyes are sealed shut. After a week, the babies grow a fine covering of fur. By two weeks, the their ears and eyes open, and they can then leave the nest to nibble food and explore the cage. If babies wander off, the mother mouse will carry them back to their nest.

More Than One Year

As mice grow older, they become a less active. At this stage, they may become ill. Mature mice may lose some of their fur, eat less food, and play less often. Mice at this stage need special care and attention.

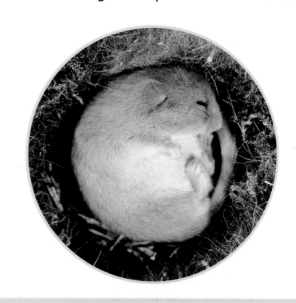

Fascinating Facts

- In nature, female mice often have litters of 10 to 24 pups.
- Baby mice may nurse, or drink milk, from many different mothers.
- Pet mice usually live between 1 and 3 years.

Six Weeks

At six weeks of age, mothers stop caring for their babies. Baby mice can feed themselves, and they are alert and curious. Male mice should be separated from females at this age. Mice can begin having babies. They are pregnant for about 21 days.

Six Months

Mice are fully grown at six months of age, and they are considered adults. Adult mice enjoy climbing, exploring and playing. They like to chew on branches and fluff up their nests. Adult mice can be allowed out of their cage to explore. However, they should be supervised.

Picking Your Pet

Owning a pet is a big responsibility. Before selecting your pet, read books and magazines about mice. Talk to other mouse owners and to your local pet store. You should consider these questions before you purchase your pet.

A healthy mouse will have a full, shiny coat and bright eyes. These are signs the mouse is healthy.

Where Should I Buy My Mouse?

You can buy a mouse from a breeder, an animal shelter, or a pet store. It is best to buy a **purebred** fancy mouse from a breeder. Breeders will know how to best care for the animal. They will also know the animal's history and health. Animal shelters may have mice that have been abandoned by their owners. These mice need a new home. If you choose to buy your mouse from a pet store, make sure that the store is reliable. The staff should know a great deal about their animals.

Pet mice need special toys and housing.

How Much Will a Pet Mouse Cost?

Most mice do not cost much to buy. However, some fancy mice, such as teddy bear and long-haired types, cost more. Remember, supplies for your pet can be expensive. You will need to buy a cage, bedding, a water bottle, and food. You should also budget for medical care for your mouse. A pet mouse does not need to be vaccinated. However, if she becomes ill, you may need to take her to a veterinarian.

In nature, striped mice live in groups of up to 30.

What Do I Have Time For?

Mice are **social** animals that enjoy living in pairs and groups. If you have only one mouse, you should make time each day to spend with your pet. Once your mouse gets to know you, she might climb up your body or slip into your sleeve for warmth. Mice do not need to be groomed, but you will have to clean their cages often and give them fresh food and water at least once a day.

Fascinating Facts

- Mice are part of the rodent family. There are 1,687 species of rodents—more than any other **class**.
- Mice enjoying hiding. This makes them feel safe.
- Two male mice can live in one cage if they have never lived with a female. If they have lived with a female, they will fight.

Mouse House

Mice need a special home with a soft, fuzzy place to sleep. You can purchase an aquarium or a wire cage for your mouse house. Wire cages are best for pet mice. The cage should have a lid and the bars of the cage should be close together to prevent your mouse from escaping. If the bars are farther apart than 0.25 inch (6.35 millimeters), the mouse may climb or wriggle out. Mice enjoy chewing on the bars. Be sure the bars are made of metal. A mouse can **gnaw** through plastic or wood bars. It is a good idea to put a chew stick or some cardboard inside the cage for your pet to chew.

The bottom of the cage should be solid and lined with wood chips. The cage should have some fuzzy cotton or fabric inside so that your mouse can make a nest. This will help keep your pet warm and clean. Place cat litter in one corner of the cage for the mouse to use as a bathroom area.

Do not put plastic or wooden toys inside a mouse's cage. The mouse will chew off small pieces. The mouse could choke on these pieces.

Mouse food mix can include many different nuts, seeds, and dried fruits.

Your new pet will need a food dish, a water bottle, and toys. The mouse's cage should have an exercise wheel where he can run. An enclosed wheel is best. A mouse's tail or toes could become stuck between the rungs of a wire wheel. You can also add planks of wood at different levels inside the cage for the mouse to climb and explore.

Research shows that a mouse can become addicted to exercising on a wheel.

Fascinating Facts

- Mice will create different "rooms" inside their cage. They will have a different place to play, to sleep, and to eat.
- A male mouse will leave a **scent mark** in its cage to protect against "intruders."
- A mouse should not be too hot or cold. Place the mouse house in a location that is about 65°Fahrenheit (18°Celsius).

Mouse Meals

Mice are herbivores. This means they are plant-eating animals. They eat grains and fruits. A responsible pet owner must provide the right diet to keep the mouse healthy. Mouse food can be bought at a pet store. Owners also can make feed by mixing together wild rice, cockatiel seed, molasses, and crushed barley or oats.

Mice also like to eat hard bread, cooked soy beans, oat flakes, and other grains. Sunflower seeds are a good treat for your mouse. However, eating too many of these seeds may cause your pet to become overweight.

Boil water used in your mouse's bottle to remove chemicals or use filtered water. Let the water cool before giving it to your pet.

A mouse can have one or two sunflower seeds each day as a treat.

Fascinating Facts

- Pregnant and **nursing** female mice should be given hard-boiled egg yolk or **mealworms** for protein.
- Mice should not eat human food. The salt and **preservatives** found in these foods can cause mice to become ill.
- A mouse will sort through a mixture of foods to find her favorite items. She will leave the other foods untouched.

Iceberg lettuce, cucumber, carrots, apples, and berries are suitable fruits and vegetables to feed your mouse. Avoid feeding the mouse oranges, kiwis, and other **acidic** foods because they could cause her to have a stomachache. It is a good idea to offer a pet mouse hay often, too. Mice like to nibble on hay. They also use hay to line their nests.

A pet mouse must be fed daily. To know how much food your mouse needs each day, give her a small amount. If she does not finish the food within 24 hours, feed her less. Every day, you should remove any uneaten food and replace it with fresh food. Your mouse needs fresh water daily, too.

Wash fruits and vegetables well to remove harmful chemicals that could make a pet mouse ill.

Small and Furry

Most mice have similar features. They have excellent hearing, long tails to help keep their balance, long noses, split upper lips, and fur to stay warm.

■ MOUSE

A mouse's fur keeps them warm and clean. The fur can be short or long, curly, or sleek and satiny. Mice spend plenty of time washing and cleaning their fur.

Mice have a long tail that helps them balance as they walk. The tail can also grip objects.

Mice use their paws to eat and clean their body. Mice also use their paws to climb, play, and build nests. Their front paws have four toes, while their back paws have five toes.

Mice have very good hearing. This helps them sense danger. Mice can hear sounds humans cannot hear. Some mice have very small ears and others have large, wide ears.

Mice have **incisors** that never stop growing. They gnaw on objects to keep these teeth short. Mice use their back teeth to grind food into small pieces.

Mice have whiskers that point in all directions to help them feel around a room. Their whiskers can help them to find their way in the dark. Whiskers also let mice know if they can fit in a small space or through a hole.

Mice have a good sense of smell. This helps them find food and sense danger. Mice twitch their nose when they smell something.

Mouse Makeover

Mice spend much of their time cleaning and grooming their ears, fur, face, tail, and toes. They do not to be groomed by their owner. However, some owners enjoy brushing their pet with a small, soft toothbrush. Sometimes, a pet mouse will have an unpleasant scent. You may need to bathe the animal. Special mouse grooming products and shampoos can be bought at pet stores.

It is important to keep a mouse's teeth healthy. To do this, mice can chew on dried tree branches and special chew sticks that can be purchased at pet stores.

Mouse owners should trim their pet's nails with special nail clippers from a pet store.

A mouse will rub his paws quickly over his body to groom and remove dirt from his fur.

To keep your mouse looking and smelling his best, you must clean out his cage every week. To do this, replace the wood chips on the bottom of the cage. You should also replace the bedding and remove all old food. About once a month, empty your pet's cage and scrub it with soap and water. Then, rinse the cage well and put in new wood chips and bedding.

When cleaning a mouse's cage, be sure to remove toys to be cleaned, too.

Fascinating Facts

- Gnawing on hard seeds and dry bread will help keep your pet's teeth from growing too long. It will also keep them healthy.
- Mice have no fur on their feet, tail, or ears.

Healthy and Happy

A healthy mouse is alert and active. She will be playful, too. When a mouse is ill, she will not play often. She will sleep for many hours and will not want to be held.

Once you get to know your mouse, you will be able to tell if she is not feeling well. Watch to see if her behavior has changed or if she is sleeping more often. If the mouse has stopped eating or if you can you see any visible scars or changes to her fur, she may be ill.

Mice enjoy hiding. It makes them feel safe and secure.

▥ Sometimes mice groom each other. One mouse may nibble on another mouse's fur.

Common signs that a mouse is ill include sneezing, coughing, difficulty breathing, weight loss, **chattering**, or singing, and sleeping more often.

Always have an adult help when treating a sick pet. If you have more than one mouse, separate the ill mouse from the others. Every day, check your mouse for mites or fleas. Also check for scabs or sores around her eyes and nose, or lumps on her body. It is important to take a sick mouse to the veterinarian immediately.

Use a soft, clean towel to pick up an ill or injured mouse. Make sure your pet feels safe and warm at all times.

Some mice enjoy curling up in small warm places, such as a shirt pocket.

Fascinating Facts

- If your mouse is scratching her body often, she may have fleas or **parasites**. You can put a small piece of masking tape on the mouse's paws to keep her from scratching too hard.
- Chattering in mice is a sign of breathing problems. A veterinarian can give the mouse medicine that will clear the problem in one or two days.

Mouse Behavior

Coming to a new home may be stressful for a mouse. There are many new smells, sounds, and sights that can frighten your pet. Most mice will hide away when they first reach their new home. Give the mouse a few days to adjust to his surroundings. In the meantime, watch how he plays or eats. Try not to let too many people near the cage for the first few days.

After a few days, introduce yourself to the mouse by putting your hand carefully and slowly inside his cage. Keep your hand very still, and hold out a small piece of food. The mouse will smell your hand and the food. He even might nibble on the food. Do not move your hand away quickly or make sudden movements. This may frighten the mouse.

Supervise your mouse if you let him outside of his cage. Make sure he does not chew on electrical cords or become trapped behind furniture.

Under supervision mice can be handled by children of all ages.

Pet Peeves

Mice do not like:
- being held
- loud noises
- acidic fruits
- fast or jerky movements

As your mouse becomes more comfortable, he may begin climbing on your hand. Keep your hand flat. After a while, you can take a few slow steps away from the cage with the mouse in your hand.

Remember that your mouse thinks of you as a big climbing tree. Do not be surprised if he climbs up your arm or even inside your shirt-sleeves. The mouse may be very shy or scared. Be patient if he does not want to come out of hiding. Mice that are frightened or stressed may bite, so remember not to surprise your new pet.

Most mice are gentle animals, making them a great pet for children.

Fascinating Facts

- Male mice "sing" songs for their mates. They make songlike sounds when they are happy or are alerting other mice to danger. People usually cannot hear these songs.
- Some pet mice enjoy having their back and the space between their ears gently rubbed or scratched.

Mouse Tales

Mice have been kept as pets for hundreds of years. They have been featured as characters in cartoons, books, **folklore**, and movies. The best-known mouse is Mickey Mouse. Mickey is the symbol for the Walt Disney Company and is recognized in almost every country around the world. Mickey's first cartoon was *Steamboat Willie*, released in 1928.

Many **animators** use mice in their cartoons. Other well-known animated mice have included Mighty Mouse, Speedy Gonzales, and Jerry from the *Tom and Jerry Show*.

Many books have featured mice as characters, such as Reepicheep the talking mouse in *Prince Caspian* by C.S. Lewis. Aesop wrote many **fables** about mice, too. *The Town Mouse and the Country Mouse* and *The Lion and the Mouse* are two fables that feature mice.

Walt Disney was the original voice of Mickey Mouse.

Fascinating Facts

- A mouse lived in the garbage cans in Walt Disney's small studio. He named the mouse Mortimer. The mouse **inspired** Walt to create Mickey Mouse.
- Ancient Romans believed that having a mouse in your house was good luck.
- Greeks believed that mice were lightning bolts that came from thunderstorms.

There are many movies that have mice as characters. Stuart Little is a talking mouse that is adopted by a human family. He has wonderful adventures with his human brother, George, and his cat friend, Snowbell.

Fievel starred in both *An American Tail* and *An American Tail: Fievel Goes West.*

An American Tail is a movie about a young Russian mouse named Fievel. Fievel is separated from his family when they move to the United States.

Mouse Musings

The Town Mouse and the Country Mouse is a fable about a town mouse who visits his cousin in the country. The cousin welcomes the town mouse with beans, bacon, cheese, and bread. The town mouse does not want this country food.

"I cannot understand, cousin, how you can put up with such poor food as this. Come with me and I will show you how to live."

The two mice went to the town mouse's house. They found jellies, cakes, and other treats in the grand dining room. Suddenly, they heard growling.

"What is that?" said the country mouse.

"It is only the dogs of the house," answered the town mouse.

At that moment, the door flew open. Two huge dogs ran into the room. The two mice scampered away.

"Good-bye, cousin," said the country mouse.

"What! Going so soon?" said the town mouse.

"Yes," he replied. "Better beans and bacon in peace than cakes and jellies in fear."

Taken from *Aesop's Fables.*

Pet Puzzlers

What do you know about mice? If you can answer the following questions correctly, you may be ready to own a pet mouse.

Q How can I tell if a mouse is healthy?

A mouse should have soft, shiny fur and bright eyes. She should be active and playful.

Q What should I feed a mouse?

You can feed a mouse special food from a pet store or grains, fruits, and vegetables.

Q What is the best type of cage for a pet mouse?

The best home for a mouse is a wire cage with a lid and metal bars that are close together.

Q How does a mouse use her whiskers?

A mouse uses her whiskers to feel her way through small spaces and find her way in the dark.

Q Can I feed my pet mouse oranges?

No, you cannot feed your mouse oranges. Oranges are too acidic and may give your mouse a stomachache.

Q How often should you clean your mouse's cage?

You should change the woodchips and nesting fabric in your mouse's cage once a week. As well, the cage should be cleaned with soap and water every month.

Mouse Calls

Before you buy your pet mouse, write down some mouse names that you like. Some names may work better for a female mouse. Others may suit a male mouse. Here are a few suggestions:

Minnie

Mickey

Fluffy

Nibbles

Patches

Marshmallow

Squeak

Speedy

Stuart

Frequently Asked Questions

Should I buy one mouse or two?

Mice are social creatures. They enjoy the company of other mice. Mice may sleep huddled together and groom each other. However, do not put two females together in one cage. Also, two males that have lived with females should not be put in a cage together. If you put a male and female mouse in the same cage, make sure that they are **spayed** or **neutered**.

Can I allow my mouse to play outside of his cage?

If you are going to allow your mouse time outside the cage, you will need to "mouse-proof" the room. It is important to remove any objects your mouse might chew. You also should be sure to unplug electrical cords. It is best to keep the mouse in a large, shallow storage box or an empty wading pool.

How do I pick up a mouse?

When picking up a mouse, it is best to cup your hand under the mouse's body. Do not squeeze or tightly grip the mouse. If the mouse is frightened, hold the base of the tail with one hand while supporting the mouse's body in the palm of your other hand. This will keep the mouse from jumping off your hand and possibly injuring himself.

More Information

Animal Organizations

You can help mice stay healthy and happy by learning more about them. Many organizations are dedicated to teaching people how to care for and protect their pet pals. For more mouse information, write to the following organizations:

American Fancy Rat and Mouse Association (AFRMA)
9230 64th Street
Riverside, CA 92509-5924

Humane Society of the United States
2100 L Street N.W.
Washington, DC 20037

Rat and Mouse Club of America (RMCA)
13075 Springdale Street PMB 302
Westminster, CA 92683

Websites

To answer more of your mouse questions, visit the following websites:

American Fancy Rat and Mouse Association (AFRMA)
www.afrma.org

Rat and Mouse Club of America (RMCA)
www.rmca.org

Humane Society of the United States
www.hsus.org

Words to Know

acidic: a chemical that has a sour taste
animators: people who draw cartoons
chattering: a gentle clicking noise
class: a group of animals that is similar in some way
domesticated: tamed and used to living with people
fables: short stories that teach a lesson
folklore: a myth or tale
gnaw: to bite, nibble, or chew
incisors: front teeth used for chewing
inspired: encouraged
litter: babies born at the same time to the same mother
livestock: animals raised for food
mealworms: young insects
neutered: made a male animal unable to make babies
nimble: quick, light, or clever
nursing: feeding one's young with mother's milk
parasites: organisms that live on or in other living beings
preservatives: chemicals added to food to keep it from spoiling
purebred: an animal whose parents are known and have qualities that have been passed on for generations
scent mark: a smell sprayed by animals to mark their territory
social: enjoy being around other animals or people
spayed: made a female animal unable to have babies
species: a group of living things that share certain features
stowaways: people or animals that hide on board a ship

Index